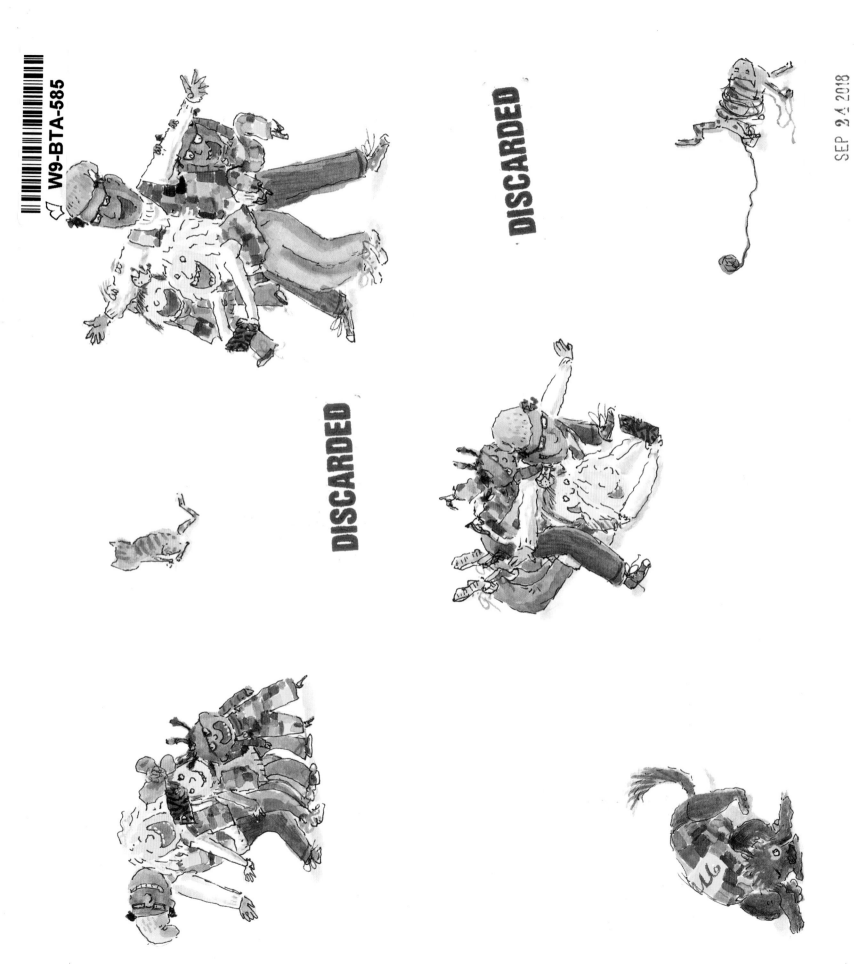

Feiwel and Friends • New York

Me, Myselfie & I

A Cautionary Tale

By Jamie Lee Curtis · Illustrated by Laura Cornell

There is no selfie in this group effort. The picture of the book's creation would include Phyllis Wender, Joanna Cotler, and my incredible partner, Laura Cornell, as well as all the talented folks at Feiwel and Friends who helped make this book so special. I could have never made it by my selfie. —J.L.C.

For Jamie, who plucked me, her gift keeps on giving, and to Joanna, who guides me and laughs with me. —L.C.

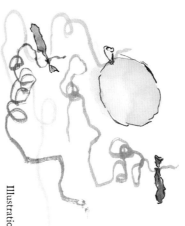

A Feiwel and Friends Book
An imprint of Macmillan Publishing Group, LLC
175 Fifth Avenue, New York, NY 10010

Me, Myself & I Text copyright © 2018 by Jamie Lee Curtis.
Illustrations copyright © 2018 by Laura Cornell. All rights reserved. Printed in China by
RR Donnelley Asia Printing Solutions Ltd., Dongguan City, Guangdong Province.

Our books may be purchased in bulk for promotional, educational, or business use.
Please contact your local bookseller or the Macmillan Corporate and Premium Sales Department
at (800) 221-7945 ext. 5442 or by e-mail at MacmillanSpecialMarkets@macmillan.com.

Library of Congress Cataloging-in-Publication Data is available.

ISBN 978-1-250-13827-9 (hardcover)

Book design by Liz Dresner

Feiwel and Friends logo designed by Filomena Tuosto

First edition, 2018

The illustrations in this book were created with pen and ink, watercolor, and gouache;
dinosaur medium; and Fabriano or Arches hot press watercolor paper.

1 3 5 7 9 10 8 6 4 2

mackids.com

For Jason Wolf, who gave me the selfie stick, the gift that keeps on giving,

and Barney Saltzberg, for the suggestion that it become a book,

another great gift that keeps on giving. —J.C.

To Mom and Dad and our Brownie camera,

our cherished few photos, our wonderful memories.

And to my daughter, Lilly, with her iPhone . . . —L.C.

Mom is old-fashioned. She likes things hand sewn.

To make her more modern, we bought a smartphone.

We taught Mom selfies for her big birthday,

me and my sister. Hip! Selfies! Hooray!

Mom squealed out loud, "It's like a new toy!"
Then she dashed outside for more selfie JOY.

She jumped in the snow
and stuck out her tongue.
Posed with our post girl.
Selfie snowgirl fun.

Selfies with Dad and
with our dog, Maisie.
She selfied and said,
"I'm SELFIE crazy!"

Hunger was building.
She said, "I need MORE."
Holding her cell phone,
"Let's selfie the store!"

Party-store selfies.

We try goofy hats.

Selfie piñata while swinging our bats.

Selfies while shopping.

Cart races get rough.

Leek light saber duels in Leia earmuffs.

Now funny faces,
we do them all day.
"Before ski practice,
can it go away?"

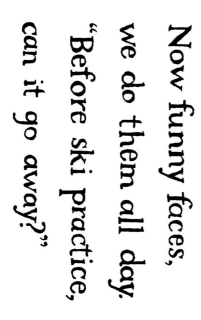

"Everyone does them. Come on, they're so fun!" I grabbed my helmet, wishing we were done.

Whole ski-team selfie.
She's a selfie fool.
Coaches act silly.
Kids too cool for school.

Is this selfie craze a big, bad mistake?
All of these pictures now really seem fake.

Mom's birthday party outside with her friends.

Snowball-fight selfies. Will this ever end?

A birthday surprise, a cake in her face.
THAT shot went viral into cyberspace.

Checking her socials: "Wow, this is my dream!
This shot will get me my very own MEME."

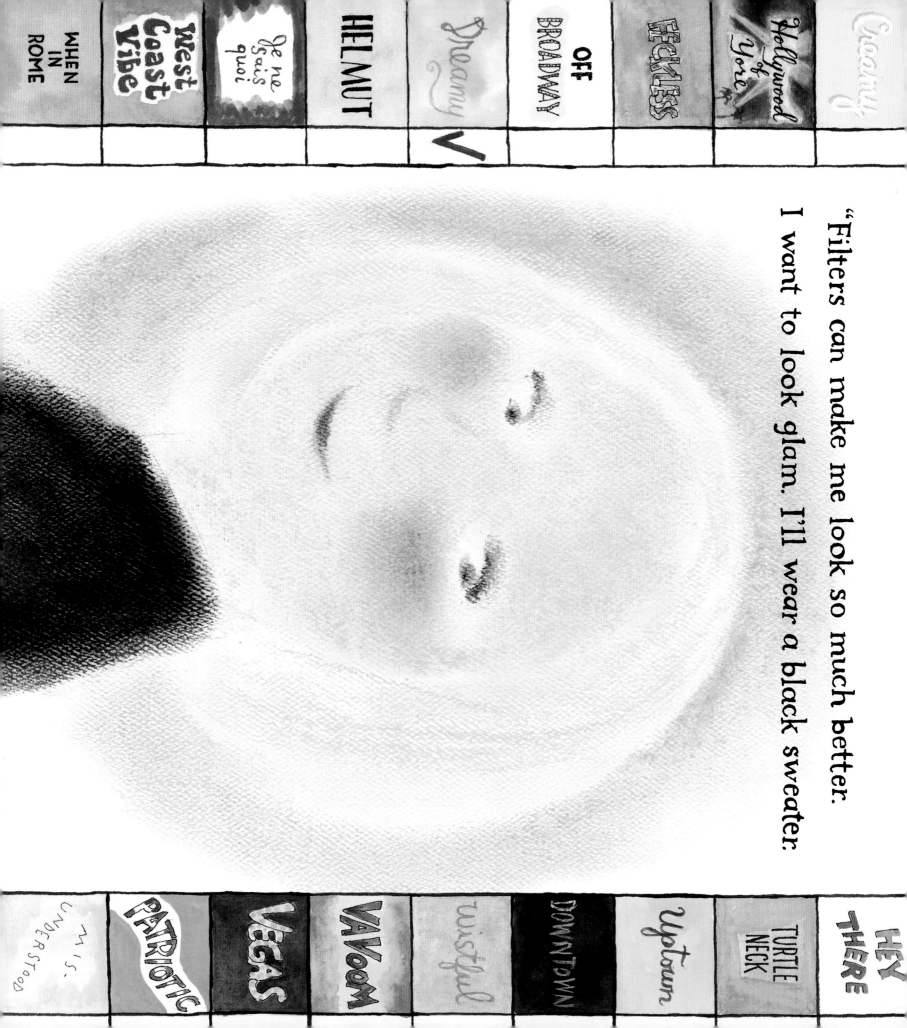

Top row (left to right):
WHEN IN ROME · West Coast Vibe · Je ne sais quoi · HELMUT · Dreamy V · OFF BROADWAY · FECKLESS · Hollywood of Yore · Creamy

Bottom row (left to right):
MIS-UNDERSTOOD · PATRIOTIC · Vegas · VAVOOM · Wistful · DOWNTOWN · Uptown · TURTLE NECK · HEY THERE

"Filters can make me look so much better. I want to look glam. I'll wear a black sweater.

I need MORE SELFIES. I'm UPPING my game.

Go grab your sister!"

Our gift was to blame.

MONDAY

TUESDAY

WEDNESDAY

THURSDAY

FRIDAY

SATURDAY

SUNDAY

Selfies in dance class,
selfies while sledding.

She even took SELFIES
at a stranger's **WEDDING!**

"Move to my left, Hon, that's not my good side."
My self-obsessed mom makes me want to hide.

Million likes later! She's a selfie STAR.

But I knew it had NOW gone way too far.

Now she wants selfies of ALL that we do . . . .

. . . till I stopped the madness.

"No more, Mom, we're through."

And Mom got quiet. She hugged me and said, "This whole selfie madness has gone to my head."

"This birthday gift, Mom, went wrong from the start. I love you for your big selfie-free heart!"

Then Mom said, "Thank you! and put it away. "We'll selfie again on some special day."

All screens go off now:

our brand-new house rule.

We cuddle and read.

My family's so cool.

And then family pile.

No selfies above.

The BEST time of all, SELFLESS family love.

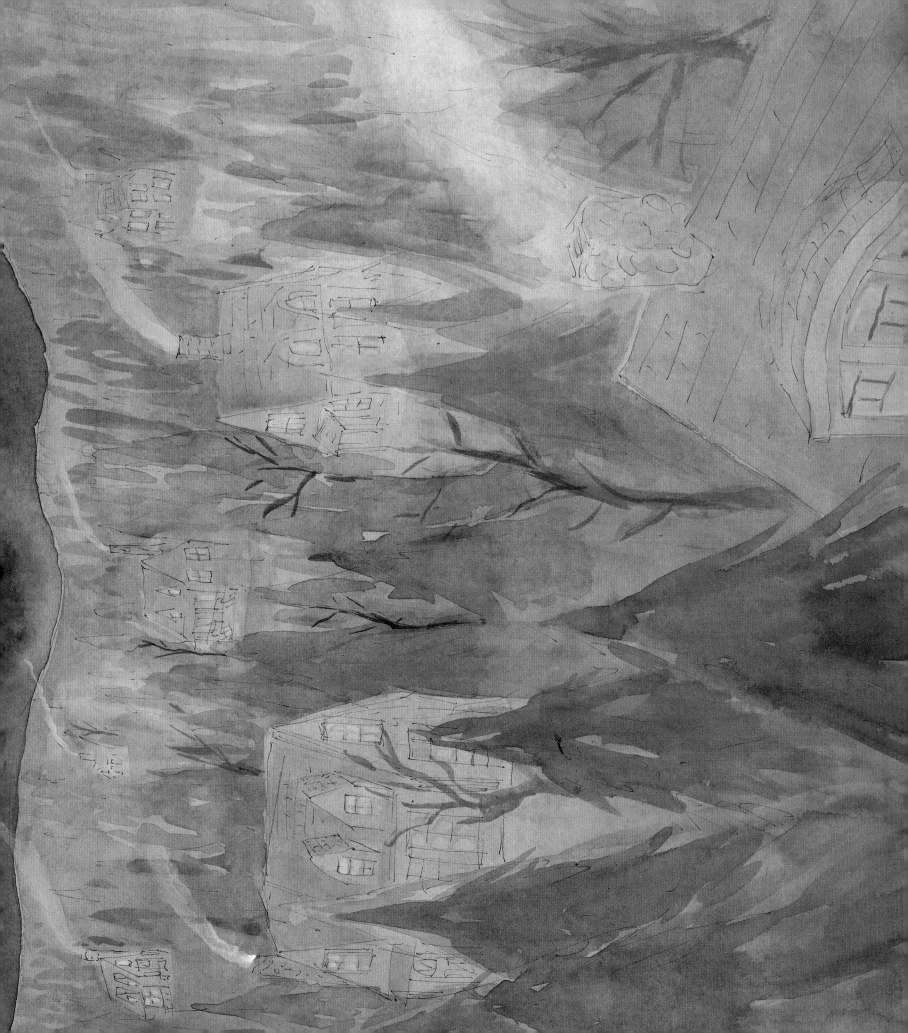

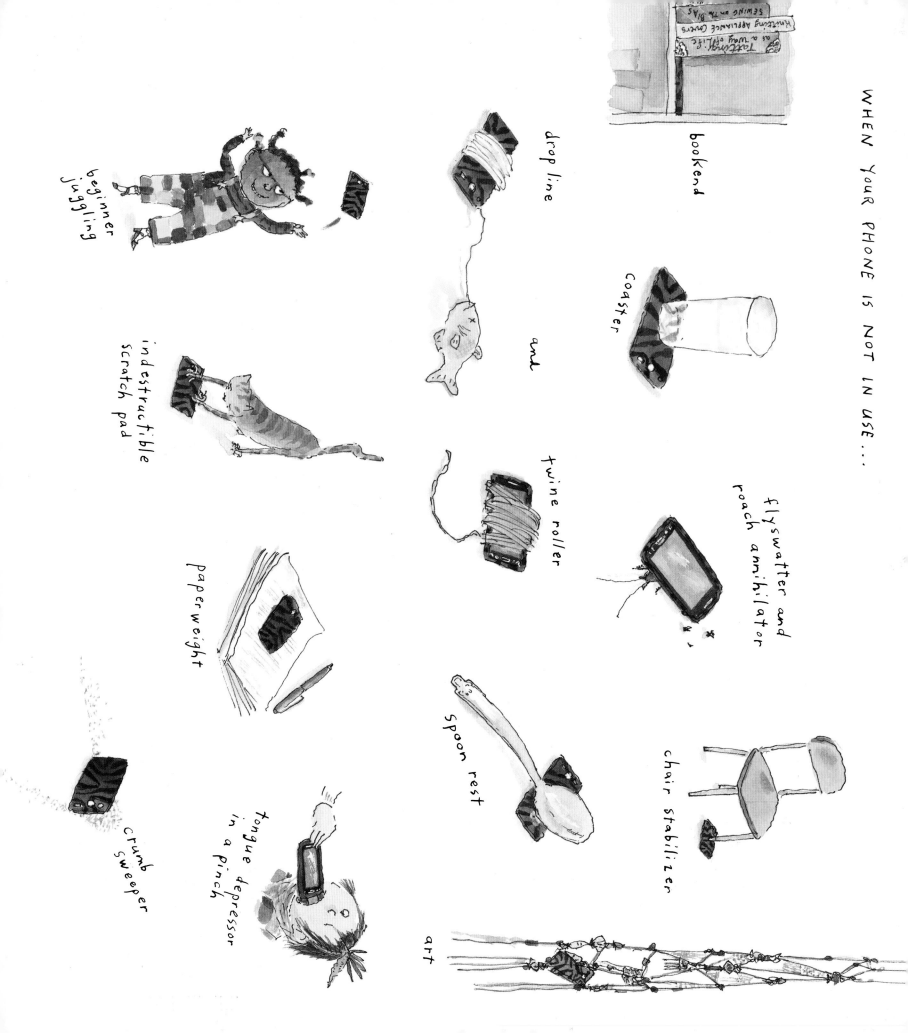

WHEN YOUR PHONE IS NOT IN USE...

bookend

drop line

and

coaster

beginner juggling

indestructible scratch pad

twine roller

flyswatter and roach annihilator

paperweight

spoon rest

chair stabilizer

crumb sweeper

tongue depressor in a pinch

art